Hot Cat, Cool Cat

LAURA MANARESI

ILLUSTRATED BY
ROBERTA ANGARAMO

I Like to Read®

HOLIDAY HOUSE • NEW YORK

Kit and Kip are friends. But . . .

Kip likes to run.

Kit likes to sit.

Kip likes cake.

Kit likes fish.

Kip likes to hug.

Hugs scare Kit.

Kip likes mice.

Kit likes horses.

Kip is hot. Kip likes the sun.

Kit is cool. Kit likes the moon.

Kip is brave.

Kit is careful.

Kip likes the lake.

Kit likes the hill.

One sunny day,
Kip ran to the lake.

Kip said hello to many mice
and ate a lot of cake.

The lake was cold.
But Kip was hot.

And Kip was brave.
Kip jumped in.

Kit rode a horse to a hill.
Kit sat alone.

But Kip ate too much cake.
Kip had a cramp.
Kit was cold, scared, and careful.
But Kit jumped in the lake!

Kip was safe. Kip got many hugs.
Kit got just one hug.
And Kit wasn't even scared.

They ate fish and cake.
And they danced

until the moon came up.

Because . . .